MARY LYN™

THE NOTE IN THE PIANO

BY

JULIE DRISCOLL

COVER ART BY KRISTI VALIANT
STORY ILLUSTRATIONS BY KELLY MURPHY

An Our Generation® *book*

BATTAT INCORPORATED *Publisher*

A very special thanks to the editor,
Joanne Burke Casey.

Our Generation® Books is a registered trademark of Battat Incorporated.
Text copyright © 2007 by Julie Driscoll

ISBN: 978-0-9794542-3-3
Printed in China

To my friend, Susan.
Thanks for believing in me.

Read all the adventures in the
Our Generation® Book Series

The Mystery of the Vanishing Coin
featuring Eva™

Adventures at Shelby Stables
featuring Lily Anna™

One Smart Cookie
featuring Hally™

Blizzard on Moose Mountain
featuring Katelyn™

Stars in Your Eyes
featuring Sydney Lee™

The Note in the Piano
featuring Mary Lyn™

Table of Contents

EXTRA! EXTRA! READ ALL ABOUT IT!
*Big words, wacky words, powerful words, funny words…
what do they all mean?
Look for words with the symbol *. They're in the Glossary
with their meanings at the end of this book.*

Chapter One
THE NEW BOY NEXT DOOR

I was walking up my back steps when, all of a sudden, BANG! I was hit in the head with something round and hard. Not too-too hard, but hard enough to annoy me, especially because it came from next door—especially because it came from that new boy, Sean, next door.

I picked it up. It appeared to be a dinner roll of some sort. Sean poked his head over the fence. His light brown hair was partially* covered by a baseball cap that was tilted to one side of his face. He had a baseball bat in his hand.

"Sorry!" he yelled.

"Dinner rolls are for eating, not for playing baseball with!" I shouted. Then I tossed the roll back over the fence and stormed into the house.

As I marched up to my room, I passed the grand piano in our living room. It used to be Grandpa's piano—the piano that Grandpa taught me to play on—the piano that used to be in the house next door where Grandpa used to live—the same house that the new boy, Sean, was now living in.

It's the piano that reminds me of how much fun Grandpa and I used to have together.

My lips began to tremble. I ran into my bedroom and closed my door. I sat on my bed, looked out the window and began to cry.

It was autumn and the leaves on Grandpa's big old maple tree had transformed into a beautiful deep shade of red. The two smaller birch trees at the far corner of the yard were just as colorful. Their vibrant* yellow and orange leaves seemed to almost glow in the sunlight.

Every fall I would run around in Grandpa's yard and try to catch the very first leaf as it fell from the big old maple. Grandpa would then tape the leaf to his refrigerator and write "first leaf" on it. It was our tradition*.

I watched the new boy, Sean, from my bedroom window. He was playing in Grandpa's backyard, swinging on Grandpa's old tire swing and eating dinner in Grandpa's kitchen. Grandpa used to push me on that old tire swing, play treasure hunt with me in that backyard and serve me cookies in that kitchen.

Just seeing Sean reminded me of how much I missed Grandpa. I missed the songs that we used to sing together. I missed the instruments that he used to play and I didn't understand why he had to die.

Ding-dong! The doorbell rang.

"Mary Lyn, can you get that?" my mom yelled to me.

I just wanted to curl up in my bed with my favorite stuffed animal and take a nap. Instead, I wiped my eyes and grudgingly* walked down the stairs to the front door.

Clayton, our mailman, was peering* through the windowpane. The design in the glass caused his long face to appear a little distorted*, almost like a cartoon character.

Clayton was always so chipper. I usually liked that he was such a happy and merry guy, but not today. I wasn't in the mood for chipper or chirpy or cheerful. I wasn't in the mood for much of anything.

I opened the front door. "Hi Clayton," I muttered* in a not-so-excited voice.

"Well, hello to you little Miss Mary Lyn!" he said as he handed me a pile of mail. "Do you have any packages for me today?"

"No," I answered.

"Nothing? Are you sure?" he asked.

"Yes, I'm sure Clayton."

"Well all righty then! I'll see you next week," he said.

Then he turned and made his way down the front steps.

All of a sudden my heart did a little skip when I noticed a certain someone walking past Clayton and making his way *up* our front steps. It was Sean!

I wanted to hide. I wanted to slam the door shut. But I just stood there, unable to move.

Sean stepped onto the porch. There was an awkward* silence for a moment. Then he handed me the dinner roll.

"My mom isn't a very good cook,"

he said. "You try eating one of these rolls. You might want to get some butter though—*a lot* of butter!"

I tried to pull off a piece of the roll to taste it but it was too hard.

"See what I mean," said Sean, "bad for eating, good for playing baseball!"

I invited Sean inside. We went into the kitchen and tried to cut the roll with a butter knife but it was too tough.

Then Sean challenged me to a game of "break the roll." We took turns hitting the roll with a baseball bat in the backyard. The roll chipped a little but it just wouldn't break.

We tried smashing it with a tennis racquet against the garage wall. Still nothing.

Finally, we placed the roll on the driveway and took turns stomping on it. It flattened a little but it still would not break.

After a while we got hungry and thirsty so we went inside for a snack. My mom served us brownies, hot out of the oven.

I kind of enjoyed having Sean around. There weren't any other kids my age in the neighborhood to play with but it never bothered me before because I always had Grandpa.

Then my mom reminded me that it was almost time for my piano lesson. My new piano teacher, Mrs. Klinman, was arriving at three o'clock.

A wave of sadness came over me again.

"What's wrong?" asked Sean.

I tried to hold back the tears as I told Sean all about my Grandpa and how much I missed him. I explained that the piano in our living room used to be Grandpa's piano and I didn't think that I could even sit at it, let alone play it.

"Grandpa used to be my piano teacher," I said. "I don't want a new teacher and I don't want to play on that piano."

"I don't think that your grandpa would want you to stop playing the piano because he's gone," said Sean. "Come on. Maybe it'll help if I play something first." Sean rose up from the kitchen table and started toward the living room.

I followed and then hesitated* in the doorway, still not wanting to enter.

Sean sat down at the piano. "The piano isn't going to bite you," he said. "Come in and have a seat."

I walked over to the couch and sat down. I could hear the TICKTOCK, TICKTOCK of the cuckoo clock that hung on the wall. It was a comforting and familiar sound.

Sean opened the piano cover and my heart did a little skip again.

There, resting on the piano keys, was a red envelope. It was addressed to me. I jumped off the couch immediately because I recognized the handwriting. It was Grandpa's!

Chapter Two
A LETTER FROM GRANDPA

I snatched the red envelope from the piano keys and opened it. There was a letter with a smaller note tucked inside that read FIRST CLUE.

"What does that mean?" asked Sean.

I knew what it meant.

"I'll explain," I said. "First let's read the letter."

Dear Mary Lyn,

I know I promised you a game of treasure hunt and I always try to keep my promises. This game might take a little longer than the other games that we played in the past, so be patient.

There are nine clues. Find them all and

you will find the treasure. It will be the
best treasure hunt ever!

And, remember, everything is just as it should be!

Love always,
Grandpa

I was in shock. I just stood there reading the letter over and over again.

"OK," said Sean, "some explaining would be really helpful right about now."

I took a deep breath and then told Sean all about the game that Grandpa and I used to play. "It's called treasure hunt," I said. "Grandpa used to hide a bunch of clues all over the place—in his house and in mine. Each clue led to the next one and then, finally, to the treasure. Sometimes it would take days to find all of the clues, but it was so much fun.

"The treasure was usually something very special," I continued. "Once, Grandpa gave me a bunny rabbit. I named him Jack Rabbit. We call him J.R. for short. He's in the cage in the side yard. And once the final treasure was an envelope with plane tickets to Florida for my mom, dad, Grandpa and me. Sometimes the treasure would be a trip to Glen's Ice Cream Shop in the town square for my favorite ice cream dish—banana split. But whatever it was, it was always exciting.

"Grandpa and I had been talking about playing another game of treasure hunt just before he became ill. When I went to visit him in the hospital he told me that he couldn't wait to come home and play our special game. But he never came home."

CUCKOO, CUCKOO, CUCKOO!

Sean nearly jumped a mile as the little chick in the cuckoo clock popped in and out of his cuckoo house. The dancers below began waltzing round and round, and the worker man at the base of the clock lifted his axe up and down as if to chop wood.

I looked up and saw Mrs. Klinman coming up the front steps.

"Darn!" I said. "It's time for my piano lesson."

I knew that I didn't want to play the game all by myself so I asked Sean if he wanted to come back after my lesson and help.

"Are you kidding?" said Sean. "It'll be a blast!"

I tucked the envelope containing the clue inside the letter. Then I placed it between two books on the bookshelf beside the cuckoo clock. I told Sean that I would wait for him so that we could read the first clue together.

Sean said a quick goodbye and exited just as my mom was greeting Mrs. Klinman at the front door.

My head was spinning with excitement. I didn't know how I was going to get through my piano lesson.

Chapter Three
TUNA WHAT?

TICKTOCK, TICKTOCK. I sat at the piano with Mrs. Klinman. The ticking and tocking noise of the cuckoo clock faded in and out against the sounds from the piano keys.

Mrs. Klinman was an older woman, small and frail*. She wore a blue dress that had a high collar. And she had a sweet smell to her, kind of like a flower.

After we made our introductions we got right down to business. There was no chatting, no small talk, we just sat down and I played. If I played even one note incorrectly she would make me start all over again. Grandpa never did that!

All I could think about was Grandpa's letter and the clue inside the envelope. TICKTOCK, TICKTOCK.

Finally! CUCKOO, CUCKOO, CUCKOO, CUCKOO. It was four o'clock and my piano lesson was over.

My mom and I thanked Mrs. Klinman. She seemed to take forever as she collected her things and put on her coat. As she was leaving she told me that my homework was to pick a song to play for the Snowflake Concert.

The Snowflake Concert was a holiday concert put on by my school each year. I always played at it. And Grandpa was always there, sitting in the audience with my mom and dad, looking so very proud.

I wasn't much interested in playing this year but I didn't want to get into a discussion about it with Mrs. Klinman just then. I had bigger things to tend to. So I just nodded and waved goodbye.

Then I ran to the phone to call Sean. But suddenly I remembered that I didn't have his phone number. So I dashed outside and ran next door to his house. Sean's mom answered the door and invited me in.

I was out of breath as I stood in the entranceway to Grandpa's old house. It was a strange feeling. Everything looked so different.

The old-fashioned wallpaper in the foyer* had been replaced with a fresh coat of soft yellow paint. And the worn-out couch and Grandpa's special chair that used to be permanent fixtures* in the parlor were no longer there.

Grandpa used to sit in his special chair and play his violin. Sometimes, I would play along at the piano that stood behind the old couch in the corner. I had such vivid* and happy memories of our times together. We would sit in that room and play music for hours.

Sean's older brother was seated in front of a computer in the very corner where the piano used to be. He looked up, gave a quick nod and then went back to whatever it was that he was doing. It looked like he was playing computer chess.

Sean's mom yelled up to him to let him know that I was there. I could tell that she was cooking by the smell coming from the kitchen. It was an unusual smell, sort of like a mixture of cabbage and burnt toast.

A split second later, Sean came rushing down the stairs.

"Would your friend like to stay for dinner tonight?" Sean's mom asked us. "We're having Tuna Wiggle."

"Uh, umm, well," I stumbled to find a polite way to say no. Tuna Wiggle wasn't sounding so good.

Sean interrupted. "She can't! Maybe some other time!"

"I'm going over to Mary Lyn's house for a little while," Sean continued. "I'll be back in time for dinner."

Then we scurried out the door.

"Tuna Wiggle?" I asked as we ran down his front steps.

"Don't ask," said Sean. "Just be glad I saved you."

❧ ❧

We raced back to my house and retrieved* the note from the bookshelf. Then we opened up the envelope and read the first clue.

FIRST CLUE

Your first clue is behind
the cellar door.
You need to go there
if you want to learn more.

All of the homes in my neighborhood are older homes with beautiful features such as carved wooden molding and big heavy doors. My dad says that they have a lot of character*.

I always enjoyed playing treasure hunt in my house and Grandpa's because the oldness of the homes gave the game kind of a spooky, edgy* feel.

The cellar door creaked as we opened it. There were a few jackets hanging on a hook on the backside of the door. We checked all of the coat pockets but we didn't find anything.

"What about those things?" said Sean, pointing to bottles and cans on the shelves just across from the cellar door.

We began searching through the items on the shelves. I noticed a small tin box, way up on the top ledge. Sean stood on his tiptoes and pulled the box from the high shelf.

We opened it up. It was filled with marbles and dominoes.

"Hey, I was looking for these," I said. "Grandpa and I used to play domino bowling together. We would line up the dominoes like bowling pins and see who could knock the most over with their marbles."

We poked around in the tin full of marbles and dominoes but there was no note. We searched under, over, in front and in back of every item on the shelves behind the cellar door.

We even examined each recipe card in the box containing all of my mom's favorite dishes—macaroni and cheese, lasagna, spaghetti pie. We found lots of yummy foods but no clue.

"Your mom has a lot of recipes," said Sean. "But wait! There isn't one here for Tuna Wiggle. I'll have my mom send it over."

"Uh, that's OK!" I said.

"Speaking of Tuna Wiggle," said Sean as he glanced at the clock in the kitchen, "It's time for me to go home for dinner."

Before he left, I wrote down his phone number and told him that I would call him in the morning.

The next day was Sunday. We had the entire day to search for the clues.

As I lay awake in bed that night, I thought about how much things had changed in one day. Sean wasn't so bad after all. I was glad to have a new friend. And the treasure hunt! It was the most exciting thing that had happened to me in a while.

I wondered if the reason we couldn't find the next clue was because Grandpa never got to finish the game. But I quickly dismissed the thought. It wasn't like Grandpa not to finish something. He would find a way. I could hear him laughing at such a silly idea and telling me to go back and look again.

Hmm, I thought, *had I missed something?*

Chapter Four
QUEEN OF MY HEART

The next morning I paced back and forth, waiting until nine o'clock so that I could call Sean. My dad said that it wasn't polite to call people too early on a Sunday morning.

Sean came over shortly after I called.

We opened the cellar door and stood there for a while, just staring.

Sean got tired of standing so he sat down on the first step near the top of the stairs. I continued to gaze at the shelves. I kept wondering what I could have missed.

I glanced down at Sean. He was fiddling with the rug that lay beside him, attempting to pick off all of the little white fuzz balls.

Suddenly, a light bulb went on in my head.

"We never looked under there," I said, pointing to the rug.

Sean's eyes widened. Then the corners of his mouth slowly curved upward. "You're right, we didn't!"

He lifted up the mat. And there, under the rug, was the second clue.

We opened up the envelope.

SECOND CLUE
You're off to a good start
Little queen of my heart.
NOW
Find a box that is small,
about four inches tall.

"A box that is small and four inches tall," I said as I thought about all of the possibilities. "That could be anything."

We opened up the drawers to the roll-top desk in the living room. There was a small box with some notecards that my mom used to write her thank-you letters. We measured the box with a ruler. It was five inches tall—too big.

Then I remembered the box in my bedroom closet. Last year Grandpa had given me my birthday present in that box. Except it wasn't just one box, it was four.

When I opened the big box, there was a smaller one inside. Then I opened that box only to find an even smaller one. Inside the third box, was an even smaller box. And finally, in the littlest box was my birthday gift.

It was a tiny blue perfume bottle filled with my most favorite perfume—Blue Dream. Grandpa knew that I loved Blue Dream because I used to always spritz myself with it when we visited the department store.

I crouched down in my closet, reached way in the back and pulled out the big box. Sean and I sat on the floor. I opened the first box and then the second one and the third and finally the fourth box. But there was no note.

We went back downstairs. Sean unfolded the clue and read it again. "Queen of my heart. Did he used to call you that?" he asked.

"Yeah, sometimes," I said, "when we…. That's it!" I exclaimed. "He used to call me that when we were playing cards. It's a deck of cards. I'm almost certain of it!"

I walked over to the bureau in the foyer, opened the top drawer and pulled out a deck of cards. Sean came over and measured the box with the ruler. It was just about four inches.

We opened up the box and took out the cards. And there, folded inside the box, was the envelope containing the third clue.

Chapter Five
TEGWAR

THIRD CLUE
You were good at this game
and the rules are the same.
Play it now and you'll see
what the next clue will be.

Sean and I studied the next clue.

"It must be a card game," said Sean.

"You're right, it is," I said.

I knew just the game that Grandpa was talking about.

"It's called TEGWAR," I explained. "Every time Grandpa and I played this game he would call me the little queen of his heart. The clue must be somewhere in the game."

"TEGWAR?" asked Sean

"Yep. It stands for The Exciting Game Without Any Rules."

"How do you play?" asked Sean.

"It's really easy," I said. "You just deal the cards and then you try to get the queens."

"What are the rules?" he asked

"There are no rules, get it? That's why it's called The Exciting Game Without Any Rules."

"I never heard of TEGWAR before," said Sean.

"It's from an old movie that Grandpa used to watch," I told him.

We sat down on the living room floor and I dealt the cards. Then we each examined our hand of cards.

"I have a jack of spades, a four of clubs and two threes. The jack is my challenge card," I said as I placed it down on the floor.

"Challenge card?" asked Sean.

"Yes, now put down a card," I said.

Sean placed down his ace of spades.

Then I put down two threes. Sean looked confused. He pulled a nine of diamonds from the top of the deck and placed it on the floor beside his ace.

"Blue-plate special!" I said as I took his nine of diamonds.

"What are you doing?" he asked.

"Double threes takes the nine of diamonds," I said. "That's the blue-plate special."

"I thought there weren't any rules," he said.

"There aren't," I replied. "These are not rules. They are called creative moves. Creative moves are what drive the game."

After a while, Sean began to get the hang of it.

"Eight takes three on a double spade," he said.

"The queen of hearts is taken only by the king. So I get your queen," I said. "That's the new-boy-next-door trick. It gets them every time."

"Bowling-ball special!" said Sean as he placed down a six, seven and eight of clubs.

"Yeah, but a two of spades scoops them up," I said.

"And a three of hearts takes all," he said. "That is my Sunday night football move."

CUCKOO! Sean jumped a mile again. CUCKOO, CUCKOO…. The cuckoo clock cuckooed twelve times.

"I'm never gonna get used to that thing," said Sean. "He is the most annoying little bird."

"He's not a bird, he's a chick," I said. Then I stole his queen.

"Hey, wait a minute!" said Sean

"Chick takes the queen. That's the cuckoo-clock special," I smiled.

Sean studied the cards in his hand. "Hey, these cards are kind of funny looking," he said.

"What do you mean?" I asked.

"My jack of diamonds has little black ears on his head. They kind of look like bunny ears."

"Let me see that!" I exclaimed as I swiped the card from Sean's hand and examined it.

There, sketched onto the jack of diamonds' gold wavy locks, apparently by black marker, were little, rabbit-shaped ears.

"Bunny ears, jack of diamonds. Bunny, jack...that's it! The next clue must be in Jack Rabbit's cage!"

Chapter Six

HUNGRY JACK

I opened the door to Jack Rabbit's cage. Jack was a small, fluffy, white bunny with patches of gray. He was happy to see me.

I always brought him a treat like a carrot or a dried apple snack when I came to see him, but not this time.

Jack Rabbit began twitching his nose and sniffing my hand, searching for his treat. "Sorry Jack," I said. "This is strictly business. I'll come by and play with you later."

I picked up little J.R. and petted him while Sean searched his cage.

Sean pulled a small wooden man from the cage. He was dressed in green overalls and a bright yellow shirt.

"What's this?" he asked.

"Oh, that's just phooey guy," I said. "He's Jack's favorite chewing toy. Jack chews on little phooey guy all the time. Sometimes for hours and hours in a day."

"He's more like a little gooey guy if you ask me," said Sean as he handed me the sticky little wooden man and proceeded to wipe his hands on his jacket.

Sean continued to sift through the hay on the floor of Jack Rabbit's cage.

And very quickly, in the far corner of the cage, he located the next clue. It was wrapped in plastic.

But there was one small problem. It appeared that my cute little rabbit had chewed through the plastic and eaten some of the note.

The clue looked like a puzzle with a bunch of pieces missing.

"Oh no!" I exclaimed.

"Oh phooey," said Sean.

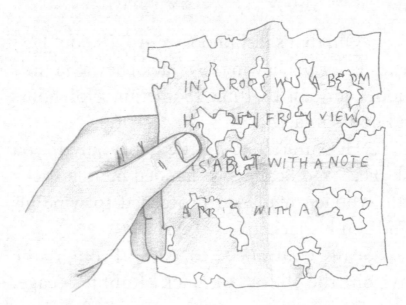

We tried to decipher* the note but it was too difficult. Then my mom called us in for lunch.

All through lunch we sat at the kitchen table and tried to come up with ideas as to what the note might say. But it was no use. We were stumped*.

Our minds were getting tired of thinking so hard, so Sean and I decided to take a little break from the treasure hunt game.

First we played a game of "break the roll."

Then we played with Jack Rabbit. I fed J.R. a carrot while Sean played tricks with phooey guy. He hung the little guy upside down in the cage and then tried to see how many times he could hit him with rabbit pellets before he fell to the bottom of the cage.

"Poor little phooey guy!"

After that we went over to Sean's yard and took turns pushing each other on the old tire swing.

Then we went back to my house and played TEGWAR and domino bowling.

Then we studied the clue some more.

And *then* Sean had an idea.

"My brother Patrick is really smart," said Sean. "I mean really, really smart. All he does is read and play computer games. I'll bet he could help us."

We went to see Sean's brother Patrick. He was sitting in the exact same spot that I saw him in the last time I was at his house, playing the exact same game. It was as if time had stood still.

Sean asked Patrick if he could help us figure out what the note said. Patrick held the chewed piece of paper under a small lamp on the desk and examined it. Then he took out a magnifying glass from the desk drawer and studied the note some more.

"Is it a rhyme?" he asked us.

"I think so," I replied. "They usually are."

"That makes it even easier to figure out," he said.

He studied the note for a few seconds more and then began mumbling to himself.

"Ram, room, b, broom...hmm ...bet, no boat, boat rhymes with note..." He took out a piece of paper and started writing.

Then he handed us the piece of paper with the next clue.

Chapter Seven

HANDLE WITH CARE

FOURTH CLUE
In a room with a broom,
hidden from view,
is a boat with a note,
a note with a clue.

The only broom in my house was the one in the small room off the kitchen. We walked in and I pulled on the string overhead to turn on the light. The lampshade above us began swaying back and forth, casting shadows on the various dishes and knickknacks* that were stored neatly on their shelves.

A broom and mop hung on hooks just to the left of the doorway.

The room was a small pantry or storage room. There were lots of things in there, like our fine china, table linens and silverware which were reserved for special occasions.

The room was also home to my mom's teapot collection. They were all displayed nicely in a glass cabinet above the built-in hutch. Through the glass door beside it I could see the beautiful teacups and saucers, some of which matched the teapots. And in the far right cabinet there were dishes and serving platters that my mom used for company and holidays.

There were so many drawers and cabinets to search through that I didn't even know where to begin. But then I remembered what the note said—a boat with a note.

"We need to find a boat," I told Sean. "But we have to be very careful. There are a lot of breakable things in here."

I grabbed the stepladder that was leaning against the wall and unfolded it. Sean stood on

the ladder and carefully opened the glass doors looking to see if he could find a boat.

"I see lots of plates, dishes and glass bowls," he said, "but no boats."

"What about my mom's teapot collection?" I asked. "Maybe she has a teapot shaped like a boat."

Sean opened the glass doors to the cabinet containing the teapots. He began naming off all of the various teapots.

"I see a cat, a boot, a pumpkin and a little house. I also see some regular teapots. One is blue, green and white and one is just plain white with gold trim. I see one with a bunch of leaves painted on it and a Japanese one," said Sean, "but I don't see a boat."

I began to search the drawers of the hutch just below the cabinets. One drawer contained my mom's nice silverware. Another was filled with linen tablecloths, napkins and napkin rings.

It was always my job to put the tablecloth on the dining room table and fold the linen napkins when we were expecting company during the holidays.

Many of the things in that room seemed to have a special purpose or meaning. They all stood for family traditions and memories from years past.

In the third drawer I found my brown felt turkey head, Charlie. I made him in kindergarten.

Every year my mom would carve out a pineapple, fill it with our favorite dip and attach Charlie to the end of the pineapple, opposite the pointy green things. The body of the pineapple with the felt head attached gave it the appearance of a real turkey.

During the holidays we would place Charlie on the coffee table and all the guests, including Grandpa, would speak to him as if he was a real turkey—a turkey that could understand English.

"How are you doing today Charlie?" or "Charlie, you haven't aged a bit!" and

"Isn't that right Charlie?" It was a tradition.

Below the drawers were three more cabinets. I opened the first door. There were a few more serving platters and a big, metal coffee urn*. In the next cabinet there was a brown cardboard box labeled FRAGILE*, HANDLE WITH CARE. I opened it up and peeked inside. It was filled with oblong* glass dishes—just like the ones Glen used in his ice cream shop at the square.

The third cabinet was filled with a bunch of cookbooks and cooking magazines—but no boat—no note.

We were stumped again!

It was getting late and Sean had to go home for dinner soon. I wondered what interesting meal his mom was cooking for him that night.

"There are absolutely no boats in here," said Sean. "We've looked everywhere."

Just then, my dad poked his head in the doorway. "How are things going in here?" he asked us.

"Not so good," I answered glumly*. "We're looking for a boat."

"A boat with a note?" he asked.

"Yes," we said.

"Well, what kind of boats are there?" asked my dad.

We began naming all of the different boats: rowboats, sailboats, tugboats, ships, rigs...

"Any others?" he asked.

"I don't think so," I said.

"What about a boat that's not really a boat?" he said. And with that he retired to the living room to read his newspaper.

"Not really a boat. What does he mean by that?" I opened up the cabinets and glanced through them again. Sean was sitting on the stepladder appearing dazed and confused. Platters, coffee urn, box...

My eyes stopped at the brown box labeled FRAGILE, HANDLE WITH CARE—the box containing the ice cream dishes—the box containing the *banana boat* ice cream dishes.

"It's not a boat," I said to Sean. "It's a banana boat! The note must be in one of the banana boat dishes.

We opened the box and lifted up a few of the glass boat dishes. And, sure enough, there was indeed a note—a note in a banana boat!

Chapter Eight
AS IT SHOULD BE

FIFTH CLUE
This was your favorite dish
when we were up at the square.
To find your next clue
you need to go there.

Whenever Grandpa and I went to Glen's Ice Cream Shop I always ordered my favorite dish—banana split. We sat at our usual spot at the counter, and Glen never even asked me what I wanted, because he already knew.

Then he would turn to Grandpa and ask, "How is everything?"

And Grandpa's reply was always the same. "Everything is just as it should be!"

I knew that we needed to go to the ice cream shop to find the next clue. The only question that remained was, when?

The next day was a school day and after school we had homework. I thought that, perhaps, my mom would let us go to the ice cream shop after school one day. But, of course, being a kid means not always having a say as to when you can do things.

My mom told Sean and me that we should wait until Friday to go to the ice cream shop. We only had a half day of school that day and she said that it would be the perfect way for us to spend our free afternoon.

❧ ❦

The school week seemed to drag slowly by. Each day I sat at my desk and stared at the clock on the wall, counting down the minutes, hours and the days until Friday.

I had plenty of time to think about what the treasure might be and where the next clue might be hidden. It was somewhere in Glen's Ice Cream Shop, but where?

I thought about the treasure hunt on my way to school, and on my way home from school. I thought about it during lunch and then again at recess. I thought about it while I was doing my homework and when I brushed my teeth. It was the only thing that I could think about, and the waiting and wondering was absolutely unbearable*.

Friday finally arrived. After school, Sean and I walked up to the square with his older brother, Patrick.

Glen's Ice Cream Shop was the best. It had old-fashioned booths and a big glowing pink neon light with a purple cone that flashed the words "ICE CREAM." The stools at the counter had colorful patterns of blue, pink, yellow and red. That's where Grandpa and I always sat.

Behind the counter were glass jars containing every kind of ice cream topping imaginable. But something was different and I couldn't quite figure out what.

Patrick told us that he was going to the bookstore across the street and that he would be back soon to walk us home.

Sean and I sat down at the counter. Glen was very happy to see us.

"Hello stranger!" he said to me.

I said hello and introduced Sean. Glen was glad to see that I had a new friend. He brought me my "usual" and Sean ordered a root beer float.

While we enjoyed our ice cream we told Glen all about the treasure hunt game that Grandpa had planned. Glen just listened and smiled.

"Your grandpa was a special man," he said.

"Do you know where Grandpa hid the next clue?" I asked Glen.

"I might," he replied. "But that's for me to know and for you to figure out!"

"By the way, how is everything?" asked Glen.

"Good," I said.

"Really good," said Sean as he took another sip from his straw.

I explained to Glen that the last clue was hidden in a banana boat dish, just like the ones that he used.

Glen began wiping down the counter and tidying the area around him. "Your grandpa asked me to order those specially for you," he said. "He told me to tell you that those dishes are for you to enjoy for many years to come. And when you are all grown up and have kids of your own he wants you to think of him every time you use them."

I started to get a little choked up at what Glen had said. My grandpa was the best. I felt his love in everything I did, and everywhere I went. I was truly lucky to have had him as my grandpa.

"How is everything?" Glen asked again.

"Good," I said.

"Good," said Sean.

Sean and I began to search with our eyes to see if we could locate the next clue. Nothing seemed to jump out at us.

When we finished our ice cream we walked around the shop and peeked under all the booths.

I rustled through the bags of candy that were hanging on the racks near the counter. Sean searched behind the gumball machine and even looked inside the metal flap where all the gumballs came out.

I sat back down at the counter and then I suddenly realized what was different. "You got a new sign!" I said pointing to the bright blue and green neon light that read "SOUP AND SANDWICHES."

"Yep," said Glen. "Ice cream sales are usually slow during the colder months so I decided to branch out a little and sell other things, too."

"Things change so quickly," I sighed.

Glen leaned on the counter with his elbows.

"So, how is everything?" he asked.

"Why do you keep asking me that?" I said to him.

He just smiled. I was a little confused at first but then, suddenly, another light bulb went on in my head.

"Everything is just as it should be!" I said.

Glen smiled a big smile. Then he walked over to the candy toppings and reached behind the jar containing the rainbow sprinkles. He took out a piece of paper and handed it to me. It was the sixth clue.

Chapter Nine
SLOW AS A TURTLE

SIXTH CLUE
Turtles are slow, but you are not.
Your next clue is behind a pot.

P.S. Pick up a package of Skittles®.
You're gonna need them!

Sean and I read the next clue. But we were both confused as to why we needed to buy a package of Skittles® candy.

I stood quickly. Then I reached into my pocket and took out some money to pay for the ice cream. But Glen wouldn't let me pay.

"The ice cream has already been paid for," he said.

I smiled. That was just like Grandpa. He always thought of everything.

The bell on the ice cream shop door jingled

as Patrick stepped inside. Sean and I started toward the door but then I turned quickly.

"I almost forgot," I said to Glen, "I need to get a pack of Skittles®."

Glen handed me the candy. "Your grandpa paid for those, too," he said.

Sean and I thanked Glen. Then we raced home. Patrick trailed behind us with his head in a book.

We both agreed that this clue wouldn't be too hard to figure out. There were only a few cabinets in the kitchen that contained pots.

As we neared the front steps to my house I noticed Clayton, our mailman, standing at the front door. He waved to us.

"Hi Clayton," I said as we walked up the steps.

"Little Miss Mary Lyn. I've been looking for you," he said. "I was wondering if you might have any packages for me."

"Why?" I asked.

"Oh, no reason," he replied. "I was just wondering."

"No, no packages Clayton," I told him.

"OK, well, I guess I'll see you tomorrow."
Then he turned and continued on his way.

ఆ ఆ

The pots were stacked on top of one another on the shelves inside the kitchen cabinet. We pulled them all out and lifted up each one to check between them. But we didn't find a note behind any of the pots.

Sean found some wooden spoons and began banging on the metal pots like they were a set of drums. The drumming must have helped the blood flow to his brain because he suddenly had an idea. "What about your mom's teapots?" he asked. "Those are pots, too."

We walked over to the pantry and turned on the light.

"The note said *behind* a pot so we don't need to bother looking inside them," I told Sean.

I stood on the stepladder and carefully handed the delicate teapots to Sean. But we didn't find a note behind any of the teapots. So, with great care, we placed them all back where we found them.

Things were going a lot slower than we had planned. "Slow as a turtle," as Grandpa used to say.

Sean was beginning to get restless so we went outside to play for awhile. We visited Jack Rabbit. It was chilly so he was burrowed in his little room at the back of the cage. But he came right out when he saw that I had brought him a carrot.

After that we kicked a soccer ball around. Then we jumped in the big pile of leaves that Sean's dad had raked. It was a beautiful, sunny day and I could smell the leaves that were all around us. It smelled just like fall. I told Sean how I used to always try to catch the first leaf as it fell from the big old maple.

Sean decided to invent a new game for us to play. He called it the "leaf game." We both raced around the tree and tried to see who could catch the most leaves before they hit the

ground. It was a little different from my old tradition, but still a lot of fun.

When we were finished playing the leaf game Sean and I took turns pushing each other on the tire swing.

Each time Sean pushed me higher on the swing I was able to see more and more of my backyard. First I could see Jack Rabbit's cage and the back porch. When I went up a little higher I could see the walkway leading up to the porch. I swung even higher and I saw the big clay pots that stood on either side of the walkway. *Pots, hmm...* I thought.

"Pots!" I yelled. "I see pots!"

Sean slowed the tire swing to a halt. I jumped off and then we raced over to my backyard.

Behind one of the pots we found a little clay turtle.

"That's the turtle that we hide our house key in," I told Sean. "It has to be in there."

We opened up the shell, and sure enough, tucked inside the turtle was the seventh clue.

Chapter Ten
SKITTLES® FOR RIDDLES

SEVENTH CLUE
There is a man dressed in blue.
He brings things to you.
He arrives every day at
a quarter to two.

Pay him with Skittles®
to find your next riddle.

We studied the clue.

"A man dressed in blue. It must be Clayton, our mailman!" I said. "He arrives every day at a quarter to two, just like clockwork. And he loves Skittles®.

"Grandpa used to always leave Skittles® in the mailbox for him," I continued. "That must be why he keeps asking me for a package. I'm supposed to pay him with a package of Skittles® to get the next riddle."

Clayton had already come by that day and the next day was Saturday. We had to wait until then so that we could pay Clayton with Skittles® and receive our next riddle.

ᴄᴅ ᴄᴅ

Saturday was a rainy and dreary* day. The rain was coming down so hard that we could hear it pinging and panging against the metal gutters outside. PING, PING, PUTTER, PUTTER. It sounded like Sean playing the drums with my mom's pots.

We sat patiently in the living room, peering out the window, waiting for a quarter to two, waiting for Clayton to walk up my front steps. I was worried about Clayton trudging* around in the pouring rain.

TICKTOCK, TICKTOCK. We passed the time by playing TEGWAR and domino bowling.

Then Sean sat on the couch and flipped through a magazine while I played the piano. He liked it when I played "Chopsticks" the best. Grandpa always liked that song, too.

It was finally a quarter to two. But there was no sign of Clayton. He was late! *But Clayton was never late*, I thought.

I started to panic because my piano lesson was at three o'clock. If Clayton didn't arrive soon, I might miss him. I might be in the middle of my piano lesson when he arrived. Then I would have to wait an entire week because, on weekdays, I was usually in school when he delivered the mail.

Sean and I paced back and forth and took turns looking out the window. Finally, over an hour later, at five minutes to three, we heard footsteps on the front porch.

I rushed to the door and opened it. It was Clayton. He was wearing a big blue rain slicker that was all shiny and wet. He pulled off his hood and wiped the water from his face.

"Clayton!" I said. "We've been waiting for you!"

"Sorry," he said. "This weather has set me back a little.

"I have your package," I told him as I held out the Skittles®.

He was delighted. He took the candy and placed it in the front flap of his mailbag.

"And I have something for you little Miss Mary Lyn," he said. "I've been carrying this thing around for weeks." He reached in his mailbag, pulled out a brown envelope, and handed it to me.

"Well, I'm running late," he said.

He thanked Sean and me for the Skittles® and we thanked him for our next riddle. Then he ventured* back out into the stormy, wet weather.

Inside the envelope we found an old-fashioned key that was attached to a string, and a piece of paper.

"Hmm, I wonder what the key is for," I said as I examined it. "It looks really old."

Sean pulled the piece of paper from the envelope and we read the next clue.

Chapter Eleven
THE WORKER MAN

EIGHTH CLUE
The dancers there are very good,
and the man would chop
real wood if he could.

Hmm... a man who chops wood, dancers who are good?

Suddenly! CUCKOO, CUCKOO, CUCKOO. The clock struck three.

With wide eyes, Sean and I both turned toward the clock.

"The cuckoo clock!" we yelled.

The chick had just gone back inside his little cuckoo house. The dancers completed their waltz and the worker man rested.

We stood on the couch and examined the clock closely, looking for the next clue.

"There it is!" I exclaimed, pointing to the little bitty folded up piece of paper. It was wedged between the two little bitty logs that the worker man was pretending to chop.

But there was one *little bitty* problem. The worker man's axe was resting on the piece of paper. And the paper was stuck in between the logs.

We couldn't pull the note out until the worker man began to chop wood again. We couldn't pull the note out until four o'clock.

I looked up and saw Mrs. Klinman coming up the front steps. She was always prompt*, even in the rain. And then I remembered that she wasn't as efficient* when it came to leaving.

"We might not be able to get the note until five o'clock," I told Sean. "I'll call you when Mrs. Klinman leaves."

Mrs. Klinman entered, took off her raincoat and motioned for me to be seated so that we could begin our lesson.

Sean put on his coat and hurried out the door into the pouring rain.

TICKTOCK, TICKTOCK. *My piano
lessons seem to always come at the worst
possible time*, I thought.

My hands flew across the keyboard
as I played the "Princess Waltz." I was usually
shy, but for some reason, when I played
the piano my shyness went completely away. It
was like I was a different person, confident and

focused on what I was doing. Mrs. Klinman seemed pleased.

"Have you chosen a song for the Snowflake Concert yet?" she asked me.

I still hadn't figured out a way to tell Mrs. Klinman that I didn't plan on going so I put her off again.

"Not yet," I replied. "I need to think about it some more."

❦ ❦

CUCKOO, CUCKOO, CUCKOO, CUCKOO. When the little chick finally popped out of his house again, I was still sitting at the piano with Mrs. Klinman. She had, apparently, lost track of the time. But the old, reliable clock reminded her that our lesson was over.

I jumped up and peered at the clock. *Darn*! The worker man was done chopping wood again for another hour.

At five minutes to five o'clock, Sean and I stood ready, waiting for the little chick to pop out of his house and for the dancers to begin dancing. But most importantly, waiting for the worker man to lift his axe so that we could retrieve the note.

We had exactly five cuckoos to pull the note from the logs. *That shouldn't be too hard*, I thought. Still, I asked Sean if he wanted to be the one in charge of getting the note because I didn't want the responsibility to rest on me.

TICKTOCK, TICKTOCK. We watched as the long skinny hand on the face of the clock moved to the twelve. And then, CUCKOO! The worker man lifted his axe. Sean attempted to dislodge* the note from the logs. The axe came back down again. CUCKOO! Sean tried to pull at the paper, but the worker man was too quick. CUCKOO! Sean loosened it a little. CUCKOO!

"Get it!" I shouted.

And just as the little chick said his last cuckoo, the dancers danced their last dance and the worker man lifted his axe for the last time, Sean successfully pulled the note from the logs.

"Whew," I said, "that was close."

We unfolded the paper and read the clue. However, unlike all the clues before it, the last clue wasn't a rhyme. It was a bunch of letters.

TICTA

Sean and I were puzzled.

"What does TICTA mean?" Sean asked.

"I don't know," I replied.

We paused a moment to think.

"Perhaps we need to unscramble it," said Sean.

I took a piece of paper and pencil from the roll-top desk and we began rearranging the letters and writing them down.

TICAT
CATTI
CAITT
CATTI
ATTCI
ATTIC!

"Attic," I said. "That must be it. The treasure must be up in the attic!"

⌘ ⌘

We ran up the stairs, two at a time, and opened the big wooden door to the attic.

The strong wind outside caused the old window at the far end of the room to rattle and we could hear the rain pounding down on the roof directly above us.

We made our way through the dusty room, pushing back the old cobwebs that hung in our path. There were lots of boxes and a few pieces of furniture.

I saw my old crib and the little white rocking chair that I used to sit in when I was little. There were a few old puzzles and games on a bookshelf and my large brown teddy bear that I had won at a fair once.

Sean stumbled. "What's this?" he asked, pointing to a big old trunk that kind of reminded me of a treasure chest.

"I don't know," I said. "I've never seen it before."

We tried to open it but it was locked.

Hmm, I thought. And then, as though someone hit a switch, the light bulb went on in my head again. "That must be what the old-fashioned key is for!" I exclaimed.

I raced down the stairs to the living room, and located the key. Then I rushed back up the steps as fast as I could.

I was huffing and puffing as I knelt in front of the big, old chest. This was the moment that we had both been waiting for. I was so excited, but a little nervous at the same time.

I could see that Sean was excited, too.

I placed the key inside the lock and turned it. Then Sean helped me lift up the lid.

I couldn't believe my eyes. There, inside the trunk, were all of Grandpa's special treasures: his harmonica, his violin, a music book, a bongo drum and a framed picture of the two of us sitting at the piano together.

I took out the violin and held it in my arms. Then I ran my fingers over the strings. It still smelled of Grandpa's cologne.

I pulled out the framed picture of Grandpa and me sitting at the piano together and studied it. I remembered exactly when it was taken. It was just before the Snowflake Concert last year.

I recognized the music book lying inside the trunk beside the harmonica. It contained all of Grandpa's and my favorite songs. Every few months, Grandpa would add a new song to the book and I would learn to play it. It was our very own song collection.

Sean pulled an envelope from the chest and handed it to me. I opened it up and read it.

Dear Mary Lyn,
Inside this chest, you will find all of my greatest treasures.
I always enjoyed sharing my gift of music with you. And I hope that you will carry on the tradition, for you also have the gift. Each time you pick up an instrument and play it, I want you to know that I can hear you all the way from heaven.

Love always,
Grandpa

I started to cry. I had been doing so well up to that point. Having Sean around had really helped to make me feel better. But seeing all of Grandpa's things and reading the letter reminded me again of how much I missed him.

Sean tried to cheer me up. He picked up the harmonica and began playing. My watery eyes glanced downward and caught sight of the bongo drum lying inside the trunk. I thought for a second and then I knew just what I wanted to do.

I took out the drum and handed it to Sean. "I want you to have this," I said. "And I know that if Grandpa were here, he would want you to have it, too. You deserve it."

Sean smiled. "Thanks," he said as he admired the drum. "I've always wanted one of these."

As I wiped my eyes, Sean pulled a big package from the bottom of the trunk. "What's this?" he asked.

It was wrapped in bright red wrapping paper with a pretty white bow. There was a note taped to the top of the package with some instructions written on it that read: DO NOT OPEN UNTIL NOVEMBER 27th.

"November 27th!" I said. "That's my birthday. That's almost a month away!"

Chapter Twelve
PASSING THE TIME WITH PASTIMES

I didn't know how I was going to get through the next month. I thought it would go by so slowly but having Sean around helped to pass the time.

On the weekends we went to Glen's Ice Cream Shop. I even tried one of his new soups. Grandpa would have been amazed.

And I would always try to remember to buy a package of Skittles® when I was there so that I could leave it in the mailbox for Clayton. Clayton was happy that I was continuing with Grandpa's tradition.

Sean and I played all of our favorite games. We even added a new one called "capture the roll."

We each hid a dinner roll somewhere in the yard. The first one to find the other person's roll and get back to base without being tagged won the game.

Playing the piano was also a good way to keep my mind occupied. Mrs. Klinman asked me to practice every day for fifteen minutes. I never minded because I enjoyed playing the piano. Sometimes I would sit and play for hours. Just like when I was at Grandpa's house.

And of course, Mrs. Klinman came by every Saturday at three o'clock sharp for my lesson. I had finally gotten up the courage to tell her that I didn't want to play at the Snowflake Concert. She didn't have much to say about it.

⚘ ⚘

It was a week before my birthday and also the day before Thanksgiving. My mom had been cooking all day and the house smelled of delicious pies and freshly baked bread.

Out came the fine china, tablecloth and linen napkins from the pantry. I spread the tablecloth on the dining room table and folded the napkins. Then I helped my mom polish the silverware.

❧ ❧

On Thanksgiving Day, all of the relatives arrived and we carried on with our usual customs*. Of course, we didn't forget about my brown felt friend, Charlie. Mom made her special dip and then fastened the turkey head to the pineapple. Everyone had something to say to Charlie when my mom placed him on the coffee table. "Why Charlie, you are looking so nice today. Did you do something with your hair?"

My Uncle John and Auntie Joyce came with my cousin Amanda. And my Uncle Pat and Aunt Sarah drove all the way up from Baltimore with my cousins Lee, Kelly and Matthew. I enjoyed sitting by the fireplace in the living room and listening to what everyone had to say.

As I glanced out the window I noticed friends and relatives walking up the steps to Sean's house. Like most families, they, too had their own customs that they carried out year after year and I laughed to myself when I thought about what one of them was.

Sean told me that he and his brother, Patrick, would sit at one end of the table and toss dinner rolls to all the guests. The rolls would sometimes land in the gravy or the cranberry sauce. But no one seemed to mind. It was a tradition that they all looked forward to.

During Thanksgiving dinner, it was customary in my family to go around the table and say what we were thankful for. I told everyone that I was glad to have had a grandparent like Grandpa.

And at that, my dad raised his glass and we all made a toast to Grandpa.

❧ ☙

The day of my birthday finally arrived. My mom planned a small party for me. We invited my cousin Amanda, a few friends from school and of course, my new friend, Sean.

Traditionally, on birthdays, we would wait until after the cake and ice cream to open our presents. But my mom told me that if I wanted to open Grandpa's present that morning, she would make an exception.

However, I decided to wait. I had waited a whole month and I wanted Sean to be there when I opened it.

During my party, Sean and I showed everyone how to play TEGWAR. They were all confused and we had some good laughs. Afterwards, we had cake and ice cream and then it was finally time for the presents.

I received a lot of nice gifts. Sean gave me a beautiful silver chain with a charm on it. The charm was a musical note.

And finally, the moment that I had been waiting for—everyone looked on as I removed the pretty white bow and tore into the red paper. When I lifted the cover to the box I was speechless.

Inside was a beautiful red velvet dress with black trim and a white bodice*. It was the same dress that I had admired in a catalog months before. Grandpa was visiting one day and I showed him the picture of the dress. I couldn't believe he remembered.

There was a birthday card inside the box. I opened it up.

Dear Mary Lyn,

Happy Birthday! I know that this dress is going to look beautiful on you for the Snowflake Concert. I will be watching you from a special place this year—the best seat in the house. And remember, everything is just as it should be!

Love always,
Grandpa

I held up the dress and admired it. I was suddenly beginning to regret my decision about not playing at the concert. My mom seemed to know what I was thinking at that moment.

"Your grandpa had been planning the treasure hunt for months before he became ill," she said. "He knew how much you loved that dress so, while he was in the hospital, he asked us to wrap the dress and put it in the trunk with the rest of the things.

"He wanted you to wear it to the concert," she continued. "So I asked Mrs. Klinman if she could give you more time to think about your decision. Dad and I were hoping you might change your mind."

"As long as it's OK with Mrs. Klinman I would like to play," I said. "And besides, I wouldn't want to disappoint Grandpa."

The Snowflake Concert was only a week away. Thanks to Grandpa, I had a beautiful dress to wear. The only thing left for me to do was to choose a song.

Chapter Thirteen
CHANGES

The day of the Snowflake Concert came and went so quickly. I wore my new dress that Grandpa had given me, and the charm necklace from Sean.

I searched through tons of piano books before I finally found the perfect song to play. It was a song called "Memories of You."

My mom and dad were seated in the audience alongside Sean and his family. And as I sat down at the piano to play, I knew in my heart that Grandpa was watching from his special place.

ᴥ ᴥ

The next day, Sean and I went out to his backyard to play. He pushed me on the old tire swing while we tried to decide what to do next.

The leaves had all fallen from the big old maple tree and a light dusting of snow covered the ground.

"What about street hockey?" asked Sean. "I have some hockey sticks in the garage."

"I don't think so," I smiled.

"Come on," said Sean. "Let's do something different for a change."

Change, I thought, *it's a funny thing*. There are so many changes that take place in life that we cannot hide from. Some things change while others stay exactly the same.

Like the cuckoo clock, for example. I could be pretty certain that, every hour, the little chick would pop out of his house and yell CUCKOO! And most days I could even count on Clayton to deliver the mail at a quarter to two and for my piano lesson to begin promptly at three o'clock on Saturday. But even these things can change sometimes.

Despite these constant changes, we all continue our traditions as best we can, like Charlie, the felt turkey head or the roll toss. Sometimes we might decide to alter* a tradition slightly or add a new one. But as time passes, change is something that just happens.

There I was, swinging on Grandpa's old tire swing, the same swing that Grandpa used to push me on, but now I was with my new friend Sean. And Grandpa would forever have a special place in my heart—like a treasure chest. I would always be able to open it up and look inside.

The back door swung open and Sean's mom stepped outside. She told Sean that it was time for him to come inside for dinner. Then she asked me if I wanted to join them.

I had to think for a minute. I knew she wasn't a very good cook.

Sean smiled. "Dinner rolls make good hockey pucks, too!"

We both laughed and then raced each other into the house.

That evening I had dinner with Sean and his family. The food was just OK. But everything else... as Grandpa used to say, everything else was just as it should be!

Glossary

*Many words have more than one meaning. Here are the definitions of words marked with this symbol * (an asterisk) as they are used in sentences.*

alter: *to change or make different*
awkward: *uncomfortable, embarrassing*
bodice: *the part of a dress covering the area between the neck and waist*
character: *qualities, features, personality, style*
customs: *habits or practices*
decipher: *to discover the meaning of; to figure out*
dislodge: *to remove or force out of a hiding place*
distorted: *changed appearance, not appearing as it should*
dreary: *gloomy, dull or boring*
edgy: *daring, scary*

efficient: *not wasting time;*
  performing a task quickly
fixtures: *things that are always present*
  or in a fixed place for a long time
foyer: *the entranceway of a home*
fragile: *delicate, easily broken*
frail: *small and delicate in appearance*
glumly: *sadly*
grudgingly: *unwillingly, not wanting to*
  do something
hesitated: *waited or paused*
knickknacks: *small items or trinkets*
muttered: *spoke in a low voice or grumbled*
oblong: *a shape that looks like*
  a stretched-out circle
partially: *not completely, slightly*
peering: *looking, searching*
prompt: *on time, without delay*
retrieved: *recovered or taken back*
stumped: *to be at a loss for an answer*
tradition: *an event that has been done for a*
  long time and becomes the usual thing to do

trudging: *walking or moving along with some difficulty*

unbearable: *not pleasant, intolerable*

urn: *a large metal container used for making coffee or tea*

ventured: *dared to move forward bravely*

vibrant: *bright*

vivid: *clearly seen or felt*

Mary Lyn and Sean
enjoyed playing
Domino Bowling
and TEGWAR.
If you want, you can
play, too! Here's how:

DOMINO BOWLING

What you'll need:
dominoes and marbles

Line up the dominoes in four rows of six
or as pins at a bowling alley would be
displayed (four pins in the back row, 3 in the
next row, 2 and then finally 1 in the front row).
From a distance of about three feet, roll the
marbles toward the dominoes. If desired, you
can mark a starting line with a piece of tape.
Each player is allowed four tries, and receives
one point for every domino that is knocked over.
Play up to three sets—the first person to win two
sets wins.

TEGWAR**

What you'll need:
a deck of playing cards and a sense of humor

The trick to this game is to find a player who knows nothing about TEGWAR. The goal of the players *in the know* is to make the unsuspecting player believe that he/she is doing well, all the while making up the game as you go along. Let the other player win a few hands and show him/her some basic moves (for example, pick up a card, place it in front of you).

Start by dealing the cards—however many you want! Randomly place some cards down in front of you and take some more from the deck. Then make up your own "creative moves." For example:

• Blue-Plate Special: Put down two cards (such as a 3 and 4 of clubs) and act like this is a really good accomplishment!

- Principal's Office: Take a card from your hand and tell the other players that the card is being sent to the principal's office. Then place the card at the bottom of the deck.
- French Fry with Mustard move: Take any card from another player's hand.
- Jack of diamonds takes all clubs: Ask everyone to give you all their clubs.
- Ping-Pong play: Give everyone back all of their clubs.

You can set a goal like: first one to get all of the queens, wins—or not. It's up to you. That is why it is called "The Exciting Game Without Any Rules."

Keep on playing the game until the unsuspecting person seems really, really confused. Then, *'fess up* (let the person in on your little secret). Have a good laugh and go find a new suspect.

**Note: TEGWAR was inspired by the film adaptation of the novel, *Bang the Drum Slowly*, by Mark Harris. Mary Lyn and her grandpa have altered the game slightly.

About the Author

Julie Driscoll keeps a notebook with her at all times because everywhere she goes, something funny or exciting happens that she knows would make for an interesting story.

Her greatest inspirations are her two daughters, Emily and Kerry and her husband, Steve, who is a lot like a little kid trapped inside a grown-up's body.

Mrs. Driscoll is a writer and artist. She has written a screenplay in the family genre and a television pilot for a local network.

*In addition to **The Note in the Piano**, Mrs. Driscoll has written **Blizzard on Moose Mountain**, a nor'easter adventure.*